I0684654

Walking in Faith
Inspirational Poetry for Christians

Second Edition

by
James J. Stewart

ISBN: 978-0-692-24476-0

Other books by the Author

Life Before Conception (Gaardian Tales 1)
Starlight Adventures (Gaardian Tales 2)
The Still Small Voice (Gaardian Tales 3)
Starlight Over Yosemite
Ever-Changing Yosemite Valley
Faith and Yosemite
Faith Fuel
Lasting Love

Author's Note

The first edition of *Walking in Faith* was published in January of 2010. It included most of the poetry written in the first edition of *Faith and Yosemite,* and *Walking in Faith* was published only in a Kindle® digital edition.

This second edition is available only in paperback. It includes most of the poetry of the first edition with minor corrections. It also includes much more poetry written since then.

Much of today's poetry does not strive for either rhyme or meter. This book does not follow that trend. There is only one poem here that can be construed as blank verse. If you enjoy reading this, your review on Amazon.com would be most welcome.

VISION

Vision is not limited to things the eye can see –

Vision also comes from wisdom born of what can be.

Others may insist on setting limits to their quests.

Those of faith believe for things that others only jest.

Sometimes vision comes from dreams
              or wishes in our hearts,

Others may awaken from a dream and have a start.

New beginnings have a path,
              and that's the key, you see.

If the dream has come from God,
              fulfillment's meant to be.

God has dreams for each of us
              before we're in our womb.

Circumstances do not simply lead us to our tomb.

Dreams of God are planned to help us thrive,
              not just survive.

Life from God is meant to make us glad to be alive.

Vision then is born of hope, with faith that fuels our trust.

Vision's proof comes when fulfilled
and skepticism's bust.

Dreams from God can be fulfilled,
for God just cannot fail.

God fulfills through us His dreams
and helps our spirits sail.

FURTHER VISION

Walking with our heads turned back,
    we see from whence we've come.

We try to learn from our mistakes —
    embarrassed, sometimes numb.

We strain to look into the past, as though
    salvation's there,

But we must then forgive ourselves
    to gain our future's share.

Sometimes we walk with eyes turned down,
    so not to stub our toe.

We think that walking carefully
    will save us future woe.

Ignoring what our future holds
    or whence our path has led,

We find that faith and hope are gone —
    we're like the living dead.

It's hard to lift our eyes to see —
    ahead seems cold and dark.

Our logic's eyes won't let us see
           what trusting sees "by heart."

The holy light makes future bright
           for those who walk with God —

With hearts illumined by the Christ,
           the angels then applaud.

It's not that homework's easy
           for a healthy walk with Him —

It's just without the light of Christ
           the future's mighty dim.

The eyes with which our hearts can see
           require a fertile mind.

Imagination's holy gift
           sees faith's great treasure find.

If you will dare to look with me
           where God would have us see,

I think we'll find the future
           of the church that is to be.

It's risky, yes, to follow eyes of heart
           with trusting love,

But heart's reward is pow'r unleashed —
           and joy in heav'n above!

CHRISTMAS IMAGES

What is the image that we want to see?
What's in the mirror that we want to be?
Yesterday's heroes are not what we want,
Our precious egos' what we want to flaunt.
'Me' generation and me on the line.
'Me' for self-help so more me we can chime.

Who are our heroes and who seeks the fame?
Heroes in everyone, that is our game.
Even in church, we find much of the same,
Self-esteem's hype is a Christian's cocaine.
Charges so strong are not gentle to hear.
Being a sheep seems like self-esteem's smear.

Di'gnosis is painful and yet there is hope.
Hope springs eternal and more for God's "dopes."
Setting their hopes on that bright Christmas star,

Brought "home" some "wise" men
             who came from afar.

Manger's sweet wisdom made theirs into waste,

Hope born of woman so young and so chaste.

Hope also flowed from
             some shepherds, who came,

Listening to God who had called all the same:

"Leave now your flocks and come now into town–

Meet now your shepherd
             and worship bowed down."

They wanted care being known who they were,

Found care in him knowing just whose they were.

See in the manger the image of God,

Then see your mirror and be truly awed.

Yes, we are made in that image and more.

"Image" but not the true God, just a door.

If, when you're opened there's love there to see,

Then you are who God's created to be.

'Me' Generation, O people take note,

Salvation's ours, but its not by our vote!

Self-help is out, only fools will defend--
Death brings helplessness to this life's end.
There are no keys found in riches or lands--
All the control is in God's mighty hands.

Christ is the firstborn of all human race,
Rebirth begins seeing Christ's baby face,
Which is confirmed in the empty tomb's grace.
Image of God, we have found our home base,
Nurtured in swaddling cloths rather than lace.
Walk with him, talk with him, now, face to face.

FRIENDS

Friends are those who share our joys,
                our sorrows, and our pains.

No one but a friend remembers
                long lost Jacks and Janes.

Closest friends just listen when
                we're bursting at our seams —

Only friends can help us mend
                the shards of broken dreams.

Keeping friends is harder
                than is making friends, you know.

Nurture is essential to maintain a friendship's flow.

Sometimes years go by with all the efforts on one
                side —

Then the times can change, and efforts
                flow back like the tide.

My best friend puts up with me through
                good times and through bad.

There's been times when I've brought pain
                and truly made him sad.

In the past, I've sometimes
                spoken carelessly to him.

There've been moments when I've stretched
        our friendship mighty thin.

There've been times I've made a mess
        and tried to shift the blame.

He's been patient through the worst,
        our friendship's been the same.

All too easily I think I'm doing all I can.

I must face the fact I'm not a perfect working man!

All of this is leading to a very simple fact.

Friendship's best comes not from us
        but is divinely backed.

My best friend is my Redeemer,
        Master, Teacher, Lord!

Serving God in Jesus' name
        is friendship's grand reward.

LOSING CONTROL

Some live their lives from day to day
            and think they're in control.

If sickness strikes, they take a pill
            while focused on their goals.

Their ups and downs they see as thrills
            and challenges to face,

Control's maintained, or so it seems,
            'til crisis stops the pace.

Sometimes a tragic accident brings life to sudden halt.

A criminal might heartlessly destroy what's in life's vault.

They say they'll just start over,
            and for some this can be true;

But when their bodies fail them
            there seems far less they can do.

So much of life they take for granted is beyond their grip.

As passengers, they cruise but
            they're not captains of their ships.

They manage hours, days, and weeks,
            they fit their lives to plans,

But finally, they must submit to life's much larger plans.

Control's been lost, so they've a choice,
                they can let evil win,

But that dark choice leads just to grief
                and crying's awful din.

In such a time, the other choice is letting Jesus in.

They then find peace in trusting Him:
                Their lives complete – they win.

ANOTHER YEAR

An open book begins another year,

And Christmas doesn't seem at all too near.

The football games fill ears with bursting cheers,

And quiet thoughts of Christmas bring some tears.

Can gifts be now so quickly lost and spent?

Can joy be quickly lost in paying rent?

Does God look down
                and know how much its meant

To me to know the joy that's heaven sent?

I wonder as I look ahead today–

To one more year of struggle day by day:

Will minds be focused just on making hay?

Or is life more than seeking higher pay?

There's hope in all of this I usually find.

There's more to life than just the daily grind.

One cannot see the future in the mind,
But play and toil release that bitter bind.

Anticipation is the fuel at hand.
We wait expectantly for luck to land
On our front doorstep just as though we planned
To make our mark on this our native land.

AFTER THE FALL

After The Fall Adam blamed it on Eve —
Too many snakes in the garden said she.
After The Fall Able killed sibling Cain,
Banished to Nod, never heard from again.
After The Fall we've descended from Seth,
Living with sin from our birth to our death.

If this were all to the story my friends,
God would have wasted beginnings and ends.
After The Fall there is more to be told,
Stories that come through the ages of old,
Stories that tell of beginnings and more,
Stories that thrill us and tell what's in store.

Stories of Moses, Elijah, and Ruth
Join with the others in telling the truth,
Giving foundation for God's simple plan,
Mending the bridge from "the falling of Man."

After the Fall came a chasm so wide —
Only God's love forms the bridge to our side.

After The Fall, we were given some rules,
Binding us tight, lest we wander like fools.
Clearly, the law gave us framework for life —
Pointing towards health while relieving our strife.
Faith's often sterile and rigid within,
Love for God dampened by fleeing from sin.

After The Fall is a pointer to sin, but
After the fall is when winter begins.
Soon after fall, there is Christmas in store —
Bringing God's gift to our hearts and much more.
Many are looking ahead to Christ's birth —
God's antidote to The Fall for the earth.

Autumn's bright colors are prelude to Him,
Paving the way to the holidays' trims.
Meanwhile we celebrate presence and pow'r,
Noting prayers answered at just the right hour.
Life's frantic pace seems to slow for a time —

Then shopping's rushed amid music sublime.

Christ is God's antidote after The Fall —
Saving from sins all who trust Him with all.
Death's part of life, we're reminded by fall,
Colors descending from trees ever tall,
Life's sweet surrender to Him is the test,
After The Fall, Christians give Him our best!

GOOD NEWS

Matthew's gospel speaks with power
          born from prophets past.

Mark's more brief, yet gives the reader images that last.

Luke wants us to see Our Lord
          through history's sheer lens,

Also speaking more to gentiles, not just Jews and men.

John, from Jesus' inner circle, sees things differently.

Talks apart from public teachings flow from memories.

John tells us of tender moments shared with just a few.

Christ emerges real and loving, intimately viewed.

Which good news we like to read
          depends upon our need.

Inspiration, facts, or change are hungers we can feed.

Jesus' teachings challenge us,
          confronts us with our sin –

Yet He can be calming, showing us the way to win.

Some may read selectively the words they want to see.

Fans instead of followers, its good they want to feel.

Then there's those who seek to be
　　　　　　just like their Lord they love.

On His path, what e'er the cost,
　　　　　　there's joy – and heaven above.

<u>MORNING PRAYER</u>

Now I pray me up from sleep --
My spirit flies -- get wings my feet!
It's by the grace of God above
I live out Christ's redeeming love!

OF WINTER STORMS

The stormy winds, they blow so cold,
                our eyes can't see the sky.

We walk about with bodies numb —
                sometimes we think we'll die.

We concentrate on simple tasks, survival is our
                mode:

We want to do the basic things, not take on heavy
                loads.

We know from life's experience that storms do
                pass on by,

And when they've passed, we might enjoy
                a clear and cheery sky.

We seldom think of dangers past,
                our lives are filled with <u>now.</u>

Deliverance is just accepted, no "I wonder
                how . . . ?"

Then there's times when danger's huge
                and slaps us in the face!

We are overwhelmed with pow'r — --
our ego's been displaced!

Stunned and humbled, weak and scared
we lift our voice on high,

Power's holy presence brings a peace and then a
sigh.

You and I are not alone, we look to God above.

God is watching over us so constantly with love!

In God's love we have no fear, for we can know
God's Son;

And we can know redeeming grace —
our stormy battles' won!

ASKING

Our asking God for what we want is such an easy task –

We may not get just what we want
                 but always what we need.

Our prayers for things both big and small
                 are easy to be asked,

Yet thanks are often not expressed –
                 no sowing of faith's seed.

Some's faith is built on answers
                 we soon readily can see.

Their doubts can bloom when there's delays,
                 and patience often wanes.

We know that God's own timing is
                 the best that there can be,

But we want swift results,
                 just like avoiding life's slow lanes.

Our prayers are often puny, small,
                 not worthy of God's pow'er.

We just don't ask Him God-sized prayers,
                 expecting answers vast.

Not feeling worthy, we don't ask,
               and blessings are not showered,

Yet God waits for such prayers
               so He can bless us ways that last.

Sometimes our God gives dreams
               that challenge us to greater trust:

To see such dreams fulfilled
               requires those of faith to ask.

To ask God's help with hope-filled dreams
               means having faith or bust.

With God all things are possible, so God's up to the task.

TRUST

Trust is so fragile, so easily lost –
Building needs honor and time as the cost.

Getting one's trust's an investment to make.
Breaking one's trust is a costly mistake.

Others that trust us can do so for free –
Trusting in others means trusting in me.

Trusting in God means that faith is required –
Courage is needed when life has us mired.

God is so faithful and loving and just.
God is so gracious – in God we can trust.

PRAYER

A scientific age proclaims the foolishness of
prayer.

The media just lusts for facts and people's points
of view.

We live our lives with stumbling steps
and struggle, still aware

That things don't always come by chance or
scientific cue.

So mysticism has its place and superstition too.

And luck is less a threat than facing power out of
sight.

So we want power we can understand and keep in
view.

And we want gods to be controlled with scientific
might.

A humble person gathers scorn by those who relish
strength.

And kneeling just is not a stance for those who
want control.

When chaos reigns as people struggle,
keeping fear at length,

Their comfort's sought in facts and trends
or in opinion polls.

The ease with which a life of prayer
is lived seems odd to some.

Unlike the lives of those who offer prayers
when times seem right,

A life of prayer is one that lives each moment with
the Son,

We pray and love the power found
just walking in God's light.

There always will be some who do not seek the
living God.

To focus on one's self is always easier for most.

To shift away from self control, the concept must
seem odd,

But life's a prayer for those who live
to join the heavenly hosts,

And prayer is so much more than giving thanks
to God above.

A prayer is even more than calling out in pain or
fear.

Our God is waiting to forgive, relating just with
love.

The bonding starts with prayer fulfilled,
with God forever near.

MYSTERY, MINISTRY AND JOY

Starting in a cabin kitchen God tugged on my sleeve.

Go, proclaim and live the gospel
        was the verse read there.

I was young in years and faith, not ready to believe.

Years would pass with other hints
        before I heard God's dare.

God did not give up on me. He even had me preach.

I was told this was my call, but I responded "no."

"Music is my call," said I. "I really want to teach."

God was patient. He was ready. I was really slow.

Wanting greater gifts to teach,
        I then went back to school.

Music history was my beat, my future seeming set.

Then came shock, life made a turn,
        and I became God's tool.

Faith became my journey,
        and my joy found in God's net.

Years have passed, and life's not been at all
           what I had planned.

God has dared, and I have lived
           as He's supplied my needs.

I've found joy in serving God, despite the shifting sands.

Ministry fuels hope and joy while planting Holy seeds.

Looking back, there's bonuses,
           as with God's pow'er to heal;

People taking Christ within, baptized in waters deep.

Trusting God with all of life
           does come with heaven's seal.

Joy in heaven is released when with some faith, we leap.

CHANGE

Change is what transforms our lives
          from failure to success.

Trouble comes with lack of faith
          in choices that we make.

Change feeds fear that what we've done
          will end up in a mess.

Wasting time with how we look,
          we can appear as fake.

Change that comes from growth is strong –
          begins and feeds new life.

Change that comes from endings
          brings new vision and new hope.

Confidence is born from faith
          that God will help with strife.

Certainty in God affects ability to cope.

Change is part of life and growth –
          without it we are dead.

All of this God guides with grace,
          redeems with holy love.

Change and growth in life are food
with which our souls are fed.

Jesus shows the way of change
that leads to God above.

WALKING IN FAITH

Walking in faith is a challenge for fools
              and the brave. There are

Those who can see beyond sight,
              but we cannot trust those who seem

Fixed on their egos and lusts.
              That is what they become — they are

Self centered czars of their
              followers' oft' shattered dreams.

Walking in faith with Our Lord Jesus Christ
              is for those who can

Let go of pride and find peace
              in submitting their will, and who

Seek to please only the One who redeems.
              There are those who can

Do this and walk not by sight, —
              but by faith and love too.

Walk not by sight but by faith we are told.
              We can hear and see

Miles of temptation to lure us
               to logic and safety. So

Much of our life is distorted
               by short sighted values. We

Need to believe that there's
               Someone in charge here below.

Walking in faith is for those who are
               foolish enough to be

Trusting in God and in that which
               they cannot see. Then they find

That which is holy released in their humbleness,
               setting free

Power and clearing the ears
               and the eyes of the blind.

Walking in faith is the excellent choice
               for the people who

Suffer rejection and failure and loss.
               It is not for the

People who live perfect lives,
               for insensitive ones, those who

Think they're in charge. It's for those
               whom the cross has set free.

POSSIBILITIES

From flash of birth we're taught just what we can
and cannot do.

We learn our limits and our gifts
while gaining height and weight.

Our minds are shaped, our spirits too,
by what we hear and view.

Our limits are not fences – rather guardrails to our fate.

The Bible says we're sinners all, we cannot help but sin,

But we deceive ourselves to think
we simply can be good.

In fact we're stained by sin,
and deeds of goodness cannot win

Our entrance into heaven,
but through Christ we can and would.

Our gifts and limits are not all
that shapes our future's path.

Our God makes all things possible,
to make amazing life,

When we surrender to His will, escaping from His wrath.

Our lives can soar above life's pains,
                    delivered from our strife.

My friends, there are no limits
                    when with God we do His will.

With trust in God, the path we trod,
                    when done without a whine,

We can accomplish what we plan,
                    and there's no bitter pill.

Our lives can fill with miracles and wondrous joy divine.

SOME TIME HAS PASSED

Some time has passed since terror changed
               our sense of who we are.

As buildings fell and lives were lost,
               the news spread fast and far.

Our anger rose as innocence was lost
               in grief and pain,

Yet courage and compassion rose
               amidst destruction's gain.

Our world is not so civilized
               that madness can't emerge.

There're always those who bear a grudge
               with anger they can't purge.

There's those who cannot bear
               to see a smile upon a face –

They're jealous of the joy of others
               in our human race.

Some time has passed since people
               cried in terror "Oh, my God!"

Some time has passed since all shed tears
               as terror touched our sod.

Some time has passed since sickness
               claimed religion as its base.

Some time has passed, we've time to ponder
               what we really face.

The enemy we face is not a nation or a creed.

We face a threat to liberty
               and freedom's precious seed.

Such seed yields hope that burns
               and fuels our vict'ry and success.

Our progress as a people rests
               on working for the best.

The enemy we face is not a people, creed or race.

We fight the crimes of infamy,
               it's justice we embrace.

There comes a time when morals count,
               when values light our trail.

Some time has passed, and with God's help
               God's justice will prevail.

VALENTINE

"I love you," said he, in a tone a bit low.

"You can't really mean that —
　　　　I'm one you don't know!"

"I love you," said he; I began to get mad.

"You're just like the rest, and your love is a fad!"

"I love you," said he, without hearing my sneer.

"Stop it! Don't say that! Don't write it! You hear?"

"I love you," said he, his chant missed not a note.

"Just stop it! I'll jail you! I'll hurt you, you know!"

"I love you," said he as his hands became pierced.

"It's over!" I thought, anger no longer fierce.

"I love you," said he –
　　　　echoes still seemed to ring . . .

And this just a prelude to my time to sing!

DIVINE LOVE

Disciple Paul says love is patient – that is surely true.

Were God not patient, we'd no chance
                to live our lives out full.

Our verdict would be final and
                we'd have our sentence due –

But God in fact does love us, giving facts for us to mull.

God's love is kind, for which we're thankful,
                if we think it out.

Real love's not jealous, nor is boastful,
                and is never rude.

Love does not force itself on others,
                nor give bitter shouts.

Love finds no joy in wrongs and
                will maintain a pleasant mood.

Real love finds pleasure in the truth,
                puts up with all and all.

Through God real love will always trust,
                endure and hold out hope.

Real love flows from our living God
　　　　　says the Apostle Paul.

Like God, such love just does not end
　　　　　and fuels our lasting hope.

HE WALKED IN BEAUTY

He walked in beauty in the days
Of healing sick and binding wounds;
And all his loving, healing ways
Were put to death and dark and gloom.
Then all the joys that loving pays
Came at the dawn — an empty tomb.

One day the more, one nail the less
Would not impair the guageless grace
Which came from God that day to bless:
For through that window we do face
Our God. So hear our voice confess
That Jesus Christ fills us with grace.

And on that hill, and in that tomb
So still, so stark, so eloquent:
The sounds of silent victory loom
That tell of God's great power spent

Dispelling death and darkness' gloom,
That tells of life that never ends!

ACTORS

To be a Christian actor means to be a fool for God.

Successful actors don't get caught
                at filling out their roles.

Imaginary circumstances lay the stage or sod

For being truthful to the setting, momentary souls.

To be on stage is actually life we live from day to day.

Our stage may take us anywhere, on any path we trod.

Non-actors do not recognize that all of life's a play.

The key is to be faithful to ourselves and to our God.

To be a fool for Jesus' sake's a truly wondrous call.

And even without miracles our power's from above.

No matter where the script may take us,
                He won't let us fall.

We're sinners all, but when we're His,
                He saves us with His love.

SAGA OF PRAYERS

One night I drove from church
               and prayed informally to God.

Beginning with the dinner and the crisis -- how I cried!

That summer night at Mirror Lake
               Our Lord began to nod --

The church I loved would close
               and o'er her death I would preside.

I lifted up my thanks and praise for years of ministry.

I also mentioned saints who gave and worked
               for all those years.

I found myself confessing rage
               at what seemed meant to be--

And then came prayers of silence
               as I shared with God my tears.

The conversation turned as I began to intercede.

The congregation's names were named
               and prayed for one by one.

While most affirmed God's grander plan,
               dissenters seemed to bleed.

A few lashed out, the wounds were deep --
                   I prayed for healing's seed.

The prayer's direction changed again,
                   a new name crossed my lips.

I could not understand at first how she could be at all

A part of trains of thought
                   that spoke of slowing sinking ships.

I pondered whether lust was there –
                   or was it Spirit's call?

That she should come to mind
                   amidst the prayers of members' names

Was not at all expected so I asked Our Savior why.

My life was filled enough, I said,
                   with problems and with games.

Opponents played for keeps
                   and stakes were higher than the sky.

Her beauty was (and is) a work of wonder and of God.

Her skills and talents too
                   had not escaped the public's eye.

If she and I will toil together, paths together trod,

Then she will have to query me of marriage by and by.

"OK," I said, "O lord, its up to you, your will be done.

"Will you please ask of her to ask of me --
                    to make us one?"

There is no chance on earth
                    I could arrange such wondrous fun.

I said I'd simply pray for her -- the rest up to The Son.

The months go by, I pray for her, but logic's in the way.

It makes no sense to hold out hope
                    except for faith's allure.

My patience thins, but hope's alive;
                    I pray from day to day.

Our God prepares us both for what will be a Holy tour.

SALT

God plans for us at our beginning,

But always we spoil things by sinning.

We're always at fault,

But Christ says we're salt,

So through Him we will always be winning.

CONNECTING SPIRITS

Just how do people's spirits touch?
                I've wondered now and then.

One lady's letters always came expected, since all
             while

She wrote my mind was filled
                with many thoughts of her, so then

The letter came a few days later –
              opened with a smile.

So many people think that such
              connections are somehow

A psychic indication of another world of time

And space that science cannot measure
             or conjecture how.

I only know that such events
              bring warmth and joy sublime.

Just how do people's spirits touch?
              There's answers for the brave.

A leap of faith reveals the Holy Spirit's linking role.

We know of prayer's connective power,
                know that lives are saved

When people pray together --
                it is more than words and souls.

So some of us of faith think
                such connections are somehow

A holy indication of a God who simply cares.

Such Holy Love connects two people,
                not revealing how

Relationships of joy are somehow built
                by those who dare.

LIGHT

We all know that evil can bite.

We can't always trust in our sight.

With darkness close in

We are tempted to sin,

But Jesus says we are the light.

WAITING

Each one of us that walks this earth
        finds slower times we hate.

We find our lives suspended, stopped -
        directionless we wait.

At first we rest, relieved that life
        has made some time to breathe.

Too soon we're bored, fed up, and irked --
        our anger seems to seethe.

As those of faith we turn to prayer,
        we seek some holy skill

To energize our search for goals,
        or better still, God's will.

We want to give God orders,
        but we know that doesn't work.

Our patience thins, our egos droop,
        our vision's lost in murk.

We question why, we wonder how
        our lives can stand so still.

Around us yet the world moves on,
          our wait's a bitter pill.

Somewhere amidst all this we find
          there's more than time to think.

We realize there's time to heal,
          we're nowhere near the brink.

Some waiting's ours because we're wrong
          or having gone too far.

Some waiting's ours because
          we're not prepared or up to par.

Some waiting's ours because
          we've lost our bearings and our way.

Some waiting's ours because we're holding
          circumstance at bay.

Let waiting be a chance to heal
          some friendships torn and tossed.

Let waiting be a chance to nurture
          passions almost lost.

Let waiting be a time of growth,
          to nurture faith and love.

Let waiting be a time well spent
          in seeking God above.

OF AN IRELAND TALE

A strange fantastic light appeared
          in Ireland long ago.

Two hundred years and more have past
          since that fantastic show.

The sky was lit from day through night,
          and there were none to know

What caused these waves and streaks of light
          like fiery oceans' roll.

It's said today that light was just aurora borealis,

But that belies the magic
          of the witnesses that tell us

Of fears and joys all twisted up
          like vines upon a trellis.

I wonder what was on God's mind
          that God was trying to tell us?

All this is part of tales of yore in dear old Ireland.

A land so filled with strife and hate
          that tears apart the land.

If lights like that would show again
    would people understand?

Such shows are just the loving nurture
    of a holy hand.

We greet the year with fireworks
    and noise to fill the night.

We count our years and hope
    that God will keep us in the right.

We greet and count, then laugh and cry,
    then send a prayer above:

That God will watch and bless our days,
    and fill them full with love.

That strange fantastic light long past
    may never come again,

But it's not part of life to wait or ever wonder when.

Our city skies are lit at night but not with holy light.

This year's more subtle mysteries
    we'll ponder in the night.

WATCHING

Each one of us that walks this earth
                finds brilliant times we love.

We see our lives so clearly strong
                and blessed by God above.

At first we stop with awe and thanks,
                but then proceed with zest.

Inspired, there's nothing small or great
                that keeps us from our best.

At other times our way seems dark --
                we strive to keep awake.

Our zest's been tapped, our best's been tried --
                no path seems ours to take.

Our ears are pricked are eyes are focused
                out beyond our scope.

Our watching's ache's just bearable
                with faith that's fueled with hope.

Our watching's painful when we wait
                as loved ones fade and die.

Our watching's painful when the truth
        is scorned with someone's lie.

Our watching's mad when scheming foes
        don't care what conflict costs.

Our watching's sad when dreams are dashed
        or when our love's been lost.

Some watching's easy on the eyes,
        when beauty comes our way.

Some watching's fun when laughter
        fills another fertile day.

Some watching's entertainment
        as we root for favorite teams.

Some watching's preparation
        for a quest to fill our dreams.

We watch because we're human, and
        we've learned that patience pays.

It's not enough to wait and hope –
        we watch for better days.

We watch because instinctively
        we know that God's above.

We watch because our world's a gift
        that's wrapped with grace and love.

GOSSIPS

Gossips are subtle, self-centered, obscene, —
Brandishing words that seem gentle and clean.
Gossips seem innocent, coating their lies, —
Hiding their hatred from friends' knowing eyes.

Gossips do not see themselves as so vile.
"Exposing" their victims is done with a smile.
Cutting off arms to remove little warts —
Seems to the gossips a comfortable sport.

Gossips tell everyone all so they may —
Hold up their victims that others may pray.
Gossips strip clothing from victims with glee, —
Goosebumps from cold then are shown, all to see.

Gossips are fueled by the pain they employ, —
Whispering insults in lopsided joy.
Gossips carve victims with hatred outpoured, —

Building up walls
                'tween themselves and their Lord.

Tongues are a fire, says the writer of James.
Tongues can defile the whole body with flames.
Gossips build bridges of hatred to Hell, —
Walking its path but not hearing its bell.

Gossips inflict without pause for remorse, —
Trampling their victims
                while setting their course, —
Auctioning souls of their victims to sell, —
Looking toward heaven
                while stumbling toward Hell.

Gossips need Holy forgiveness from God.
Penitence — real — brings a sigh and a nod.
Logs in their own eyes, — lets pray that they see.
Then 'twill be better for you and for me!

HOPE

Living in fear we can't cope.

Living unhappy we mope.

Trusting in God

Is the path that we trod

Because hope that is seen is not hope.

Living in joy we can cope —

Faith conquers our steepest slope!

Trusting in God

Is the path that we trod,

For we're living in joy, faith and hope.

THIS TALE OF CHURCH

(Honoring the close of Mirror Lake Christian Church
of St. Petersburg, Florida)

St. Petersburg in nineteen hundred
        was the time and place,

A group began a ministry
        just south of downtown's core.

Their mission was a simple one,
        'twas needs that set the pace.

They found relieving hurt and pain
        to be both joy and chore —

The greatest joy was leading souls
        to meet Christ face to face.

Twice these people took a stand
        against a world-wide war,

Yet while they did this held the hands
        of anxious folks at home.

They took their stands against injustice,
        hunger, pain, and war; —

Yet history shows encouragement
        as louder than their moans.

They knew full well what they opposed,
           but made their fighting "for."

Our "Mirror Lake's a special place where God has
           made a mark —

A reservoir and fountain
           at the center of some green

Has been a place where those of faith
           transformed a city park.

As saints built up a ministry,
           pursuing Holy dreams,

The love of Christ was shared, and
           some found light amid the dark.

To be the church is harder now
           than many decades past. —

Society is skeptical, impatient to the core,

But faithful folk at Mirror Lake
           could see what really lasts.

They saw beyond their present state the larger
           church and more —

By helping other churches now
           their future role was cast.

This tale of church now seems to end,
           but that's not really true!

This "church" has been an episode
           in God's far larger plan.

A host of memories of joy
     will soon dispel the blues.

Our saying "Have a nice forever"
     bridges sorrow's span.

God bless this cloud of witnesses —
     both seen and unseen too!

TO ELLE

[Written to Elle MacPherson, 1993]

You walk in beauty in the days
Of culture's doom and lust and greed.
Amidst the grief of God you pay
The price of other's praise indeed;
(And all that's best of sense and wit
Are wasted in this model's grit.)

One cover more, one cover less
Does not affect your will to sell
Your images of eye and tress
And body simply known as Elle.
You think you know your gifts of God
Though that is not the way you've trod.

Your present path's about to turn —
You're not prepared for what's in store.
You'll find fulfillment means to burn
Your bridges, yet there's even more.
Your future's bright and full of joy,
Yet with your past you'll want to toy.

The simple truth, dear Elle, is this:
The answer to your secret prayers
Is not what you expect of bliss!
It won't be clothing hems and tears
That make your public image clear,
But people's hearts that you'll hold dear.

CHRISTMAS 1986 –
FOR KATHLEEN STEWART

Kathy, musician and Aunt, and there's more,

Music at Christmas brings joy to the fore.

Jesus, the babe with such promise in store,

Promises peace to you, joy, and still more.

Kathy, shalom to you, now and all year,

Just as in singing of that midnight clear,

Cling to Him, close to Him, find in Him cheer –

He'll see you through as His blessings appear.

ON THE CARIBBEAN

[Written on a Windjammer Cruise, 1997]

From the top of the gangway
>> she stepped onto the deck.
>> Perspiration decked her flawless
>> skin – she had spent the afternoon
>> hauling in a large Mahi-mahi.

There wasn't a touch of makeup,
>> and even with a few strands
>> of hair askew, she was the most
>> beautiful woman I had ever seen.

As photogenic as she was and is,
>> it was not her beautiful face
>> and figure that held my gaze.

God showed me her heart
>> and gave me a sense of her soul.

When cleaned up
>> she accepted a drink of rum
>> and pineapple juice
>> with a mock curtsey and a
>> "Why thank you kind sir!"

I was truly smitten
and probably in love.

CHILDREN OF GOD

People seeking God the first time often are amazed.

Can it be they ask themselves that God will all forgive?

Great and lavish is God's love,
                His children could be dazed.

Walking in God's love, they're taught
                by Jesus how to live.

LIVING IN THE VINE

As followers of Jesus we are branches of His vine.

He wants His branches to bear fruit,
                for that's the thriving life.

When we bear fruit we're pruned
                to bear more fruit on down the line.

When we don't bear His fruit we're trimmed,
                and no one wants that strife.

We're cleaned already by His word,
                His testimony's clear.

His followers live in His vine,
                the fruit comes from His being.

We can't bear fruit without His vine,
                His love for us is dear.

We bear His fruit, His life in us,
                His love in us is seen.

When living in His vine abundant fruit
                then comes from us –

Our fruit's empowered by His life,
                we're flavored by His joy.

We can't bear fruit without Him,
                our own efforts just a fuss;

Without His joy and love within,
                our fruit's a worthless toy.

Those fans who aren't His followers,
                just don't live in His vine.

The branches of His fans just don't bear fruit
                and have no worth.

However big the fruitless branches,
                beautiful or fine.

They disappoint The Father
                and are sent back into earth.

When followers live in His vine,
                His words live in our hearts.

Our prayers can ask for anything
                reflecting His pure life.

His answers come reflecting Him,
                for we have done our part.

Our fruit is born from His true vine,
                the truly Christian life.

NOW

Impatiently we want things now,
        the time for waiting's never been.

It seems that everything we do
        is sensitive to timing's pen.

This pen's a cage without a door,
        and nothing's right outside its bars.

Yet from the vantage point of God
        there are no bars, there's only stars.

The now of God is never caged
        or bound by circumstance of law.

The thought of God is polished substance
        even though created raw.

The word of God is now and whole,
        created without timing's cage.

The now of God is flawless joy,
        without the need to turn a page.

Tomorrow's needs will come in time,
        and yesterdays will always press.

The needs of yesterday were either solved
          or added to our mess.

The needs of now are quicker solved
          when yesterday is in the past.

The now with which we work at last
          cannot be measured slow or fast.

Impatiently we want things now,
          not hearing "no" or even "slow."

With time there's opportunity to wait
          for now and simply grow.

When wisdom comes, the now gives way
          to slowly finding what has been.

Such wisdom finds such strength for now that
          future's joy looks back at "then."

When life on earth is done and there is simply
          no more now to face,

I think the loss of time's firm bars
          will edify God's holy grace.

When death is passed and life's set free
          to soar through all eternity,

I think I'll see the now of God
          as love fulfilled with joyful glee.

THE FRIENDS OF CHRIST

Friendship is not learned in classes,
                but it must be learned.

Friends walk with you through the flames,
                e'en though they may be burned.

Friends will know you through and through
                and love you anyway.

Being friends means all of this,
                and trusting all the way.

Walking with the Lord of Life means
                walking with a friend.

Unlike us He's always faithful,
                right up through the end.

When we're at our lowest He is
                somehow always there,

Giving us what's needed,
                and supplying what is fair.

Jesus grants us freedom, we can be
                ourselves –but more.

His way's often harder,
               but rewards are great in store.

Friends with Christ give of themselves
               with efforts great and small.

Friends with Jesus find His love's
               the greatest prize of all.

FRUITS & NUTS

When God created all we are and all creation too,

Our needs were met within our reach,
        with little work to do.

Our hungers filled with fruits and nuts,
        we had no cause to doubt

Why God had placed a limit
        on what life is all about.

Our simple lives and diet told of life so innocent --

We had no cares, our needs were met,
        for all was heaven sent.

Our lives were rich and full of joy --
        we lived off of the land.

But then a kind of nut entranced us
        with a fruit that's banned.

We think of fruit that comes from vines,
        from bushes, and from trees,

We think in terms of what we eat and not what
        others see.

Our fruit from us has strength to alter lives
and change our fate.

Our fruit's our mark of excellence -- or poison from
our hate.

The fruit of God is joy and love,
God's role for us is cast:

God's very nature's filled with hope --
God's dreams for us are vast.

The Other's fruit is fickle,
and its taste is often sour.

Temptation's fruit is charming,
but it's consequences dour.

We're all just branches, you and I,
our fruits are how we're known.

When people taste and see our fruit
they know what seed's been sown.

We cling as branches to Our Vine --
His being all that's true --

And when our harvest comes
we'll still be His in heaven too.

<u>COURAGE</u>

Courage in the midst of fear is
                vital for the brave.

Lives are saved, are spent, or both
                when fear is set aside.

This one virtue can emerge when
                lives need to be saved,

Making others more important
                than our precious hide.

Other virtues, when they're tested,
                lean on courage strong.

Honesty and purity need courage to be held.

Diligence and kindness need some
                courage when seems "wrong."

Expressions of humility need courage deeply held.

Courage from just one is a majority, and more.

Brave souls win against
                a thousand cowards' and their hate.

Courage grows from repetitions
                of the past in store,

And a brave response is better earlier than late.

Courage is a virtue that is cherished far and wide.

Those in uniform need courage
              just to live their call.

Sometimes courage is required
              when risk is at our side.

Courage against evil fuels
              our victories great and small.

THOUGHTS AT RANDOM

To wait for God is not such easy work

I keep on hoping I've not been a jerk.

There is no hope my dreams can be fulfilled

Unless the soil of miracles is tilled.

I pray each day Christ's church will be renewed.

To nurture hope is now my spirit's food.

PRAYER IS LIKE A SPINNING WHEEL

Prayer is like a steering wheel – it guides the
roving mind.

It cannot be just sent-up flares to God for crises'
sake.

To read of saints in scriptures feels like fuel so
good to find.

We move through life and care to dare
when evil's on the make.

So prayer and power grows our faith as evil's left
behind.

PURITY

When Jesus says the pure in heart see God,
It's character He's wanting us to grow.
Such growth makes pure the path we boldly trod,
While living lives amid both friends and foes.

Some see their lives as pure, without a care,
Not thinking if their stance brings others harm.
Without a humble thought they often dare
To act as though beyond God's mighty arm.

When pure in heart, a Christian dares to be
A person who fulfills God's plans and more.
Without restrictions, God then sets them free
To find God's blessings and His joy in store.

FAITH AND YOSEMITE

While driving in the valley
        when the trees are whipping by,

The foreground in a blur while cliffs
        stand sharp against the sky,

A freedom stirs inside us
        and restores our life again,

Restoring sense of balance,
        and our lives begins to mend.

Our Half Dome urges centeredness,
        we feel our God on high.

There's feelings of our groundedness
        felt from its base to sky.

Our faith within Yosemite
        is sometimes focused here,

And prayer is sometimes faith's response
        as God is felt so near.

The waterfalls that thunder loud
        can also seem serene.

Their mists so free and pools so deep
                create a peaceful scene.

A fall's intensity can stir excitement to our core.

There's fascination, freedom, passion,
                energy, and more.

The valley brings a sense of wonder
                not seen anywhere,

We walk, and hike, and bike, and drive –
                and sometimes stop to stare.

The eyes of faith can sense God's love
                in beauty all around.

For most it's just refreshment
                'til again they're homeward bound.

Be thankful for a God that gives us
                eyes to see such grace.

Be thankful for the privilege of
                enjoying such a place.

As eyes of faith look up, around,
                we call upon God's name.

There's fascination in this place of change
                that seems the same.